AF226525

Salt

Pepper

Dedication

Helena's: For Hubs and Kidlet

Debra's:T, J and D, it's always all for you

Other Titles From Debra Anastasia

Silly Humor:

FIRE DOWN BELOW

FIRE IN THE HOLE

Funny Humor:

BEAST

BOOTY CAMP

FELONY EVER AFTER

Angst with Feels:

DROWNING IN STARS

MERCY

HAVOC

LOCK

POUGHKEEPSIE BROTHERHOOD SERIES

Paranormal:

THE REVENGER

FOR ALL THE EVERS

SERAPHIM SERIES

Other Titles From Helena Hunting

ALL IN SERIES

A Lie for a Lie

A Favor for a Favor

A Secret for a Secret

PUCKED SERIES

Pucked (Pucked #1)

Pucked Up (Pucked #2)

Pucked Over (Pucked #3)

Forever Pucked (Pucked Book #4)

Pucked Under (Pucked #5)

Pucked Off (Pucked #6)

Pucked Love (Pucked #7)

AREA 51: Deleted Scenes & Outtakes

Get Inked

Pucks & Penalties

SHACKING UP SERIES

Shacking Up

Getting Down (Novella)

Hooking Up

I Flipping Love You

Making Up

Handle With Care

THE CLIPPED WINGS SERIES

Cupcakes and Ink

Clipped Wings

Between the Cracks

Inked Armor

Cracks in the Armor

Fractures in Ink

STANDALONE NOVELS

The Librarian Principle

Felony Ever After

FOREVER ROMANCE STANDALONES

The Good Luck Charm

Meet Cute

Kiss My Cupcake

Little Lies

Salt
&
Pepper

Before
You
Ghost

One

SAMMI

I NEVER IMAGINED my lady bits would be photographed as a crime scene, but here we are. At least I had put my clothes on, but all the bystanders understood what was going on.

I'd never had so many straight-faced people learn how and where I put my limbs during doggy style.

But when your boyfriend flies off a cliff behind you during your adventurous hiking sex, new experiences crop up.

And I would cry more. And maybe even scream some if his ghost wasn't sitting three feet from me cracking jokes the whole time. Hell, for all I know, he might have even finished as a ghost.

"Do you want me to help them find the disaster area tape? Or do you think people can just judge that from your granny panties? I bet we can fashion a thong out of the tape. Save a little of your rep."

I had to wait for the detective to finish up his last batch of photos before I could hiss in Evan's direction, "I wear granny panties when we hike so I don't get wedgies. You know that."

"Miss? Everything okay?" The cop seemed worried about me. I should possibly be more worried about me. Maybe it was shock mixed with the energy drink Evan had passed to me just before the incident.

"Using sex as a weapon, huh?" Ghost Evan gave me a wink.

I pursed my lips and gave him a hard stare.

"You know, I kinda love this. You can't give me attitude. People will think you're crazy."

He was enjoying this. His almost see-through handsome face was flashing his token smile. Damn, his giant pearly whites and devilish dimples. He got out of a lot of trouble with those things. And now he's getting me into a lot of trouble *with* them.

I bit my lips from the inside to keep all my comebacks from coming out of my mouth. We fought. It's what we did. I had a temper and he had an attitude. Our makeup sex was off the charts. Half the time we were giving each other a hard time just to get to the good times.

I overheard the closest group of cops pontificating about the situation that had recently occurred as I glared at Evan.

"I mean, that's another clear video. She's on her hands and knees and when they, um… finish, it appears that her orgasm is so strong that it literally launches him off the cliff like a cannon."

I turned my head just as the three cops shifted to face me.

We all had the most awkward eye contact in the history of human existence.

One cleared his throat, the other adjusted his belt, and the third was blushing so hard his ears were red.

"Your pussy blew me off the cliff of Lover's Peak?" Evan was bent over laughing. They couldn't hear him, but I could. He was pissing me off.

Cliff fighting was a bad idea. Cliff sex was worse.

We got each other like that. Hot and bothered. I would grab the front of his shirt and then he would grab me by my ass and haul me to him.

And his stupid jaw was so well-defined. I had bitten it. Well, of course, next thing you know we were pulling each other's clothes off. In a highly public place. On the edge of a cliff.

The red-eared cop approached. "I'm supposed to find out if you have any injuries?"

I shook my head, lips still in a restraint with my teeth.

"Okay, well, we have various videos from numerous sources that clearly show no malicious intent on your part. I mean, our captain has to take a look. And maybe the coroner? We can't get your boyfriend's body off the cliff right now. The rescue team has to come out with the proper equipment. They said they can come by around lunchtime tomorrow. They're on a call. The boys and I are going to try to tarp up the body." He jammed his hands into his pockets as his forehead joined his ears in their red color.

"So I can go?" That seemed wrong somehow. But Evan

had already stood and was brushing off his ghost pants. That was always his signal that he wanted to leave.

Red Ears seemed reluctant to answer that question and looked over his shoulder twice. Finally, he shrugged and showed me his teeth like he was smiling for his preschool picture.

I stood, too, joining Evan.

"Don't forget your fanny pack. And your hat." Evan tried to grab both for me. His finger rustled them a little, but he was unable to grab them. I did it instead.

It was the first time his mood dampened. The wicked, semi-opaque sparkle left his eyes briefly.

I needed to hike back down the mountain. I was grateful that we took my car and not his earlier—at least I had the keys in my fanny pack. The hike down was much shorter than the hike up had been. Of course, Evan and I had stopped to fight and then kiss and then fight some more on the way up.

"What were we even arguing about?" I pointed to a distinctive row of trees that had the bark smoothed off from either animals or weather. He'd pressed me against that tree and kissed the hell out of me earlier while we dry humped each other, back when he was alive.

"I don't remember. You were angry, which makes you even hotter. And then your nose flared a bit and it was over for me. Whatever it was, just remembering it makes me horn…" he trailed off and looked down. I looked down with him. We were like two dogs that had their favorite toy taken away for misbehaving. The silence filled itself with the sounds of nature. Birds chirped and a couple of

squirrels made that annoying clicking noise.

"Is it...doing anything?" I tried to squint to see if his ghost pants had moved in any way.

"Holy crap. Do not squint at my dick. Can you not? I mean, try to look a little impressed or something." He gestured to his crotch.

I looked from his face to my hand to his crotch once, twice, and by the third time, Evan had resigned himself to what must have been clearly obvious.

I wanted to touch it.

I stretched out my hand, palm up, and stepped closer to him. I held my breath. His ghost eyes were wide and slightly untrusting, which was fair. Neither of us knew what was going to happen if I managed to cup his ghost junk.

Closer still. And then, just as I was about to make contact or slide right through his body, we both heard the cops jingling down the mountain.

"Nice shot, man. I didn't think you could cover a whole body with one tarp like that. If there was a body covering event in the Olympics, you'd get at least a bronze, Michigan." We heard the telltale sound of two palms slapping together in a high-five. It was followed by birds cawing their annoyance and squirrels nattering angrily.

Evan's Adam's apple bobbed up and down as we overheard the police talking about his corpse.

"Yeah, well, you can't leave a man uncovered like that. His twig and berries were out." They came into the clearing just as the pants adjusting cop finished up his observation.

I pulled my hand away from Evan's crotch. It was weird

that his ghost was fully dressed, but his body was naked as the day he was born. Maybe there was such a thing as ghost modesty?

"You okay, miss?"

I took a deep breath. Maybe this would all hit me soon. Maybe my shock was a real thing that was just hovering on the edge of my sanity.

"You know what? I think maybe I shouldn't drive home. Would it be cool if you dropped me off? I'll come back later to get my car."

Red Ears nodded quickly. "Yeah, of course. You know what? Michigan here can drive your car home, save you the trouble later."

"Thanks. I feel like this hasn't hit me yet, you know?"

"That makes sense." They went from joking about Evan's body to being understanding about my concerns at the snap of the fingers. They must bounce from emotion to emotion all day, every day. Like squirrels hopping from tree to tree, or electrical pole to electrical pole.

"We'll take you home. No problem." They all handed me business cards. I didn't know cops even carried them.

I made sure Evan was able to come with me. He sat in the back of the squad car as I sat up front with Red Ears. I noticed that the back car door never opened, yet Evan was still present. We'd have some things to discuss tonight, for sure.

I GOT READY for the evening like I always did. Took a

shower, washed my face, used my toner, put on my night cream, and made sure my armpits were hairless, as well as my lady business. I made Evan promise he'd stay in the living room since locking the bathroom door was pointless. He could just walk through it if he wanted.

Evan struggled to pick up his toothbrush next to mine.

"Should we both be screaming at this point?" His hand passed through the handle of the brush yet again.

I folded my arms across my chest. Maybe I would wake up and the whole thing would be a giant hairy nightmare.

"Does it feel like anything when you move through stuff?"

He shrugged his massive shoulders. There was a reason we were still together. His beautiful shoulders were like eighty percent of why I put up with the fighting. His pretty face was another ten percent, his giant sex pistol another nine percent, and the final one percent was reserved for his personality and killer sense of humor. No pun intended.

"I mean, I guess it tickles a little?" His hands fell to his sides, clearly giving up.

"Let's sleep on it. Maybe we'll both feel better in the morning." I wanted to offer him some comfort, but I was concerned that giving him a hug right now and walking through him would freak him out more than he already was. And that I would finally lose what little was left of my sanity.

I turned and walked to the bed, pulling the covers back for the both of us. He hopped in on his side, but the bed didn't register his weight. I got in and covered us both with a blanket. It went right through him. I was under the covers, and he was on top of them. I had to move the pillow for him, too, because his head would sink about halfway into it and he said it was giving him a headache. I wasn't sure he could actually get a headache since he wasn't alive, but I didn't feel like addressing that was a good plan.

He was staying on the bed, though, and I pointed it out to him, "Well, you have some sort of control over gravity, otherwise you would sink straight through the floor."

I reached over to the melatonin bottle and took a gummy, then shook out a second one. I was going to need a little help falling asleep tonight.

Two

EVAN

W ELL, CLOSING MY eyes was pointless. I could see through my eyelids. I was dead. I mean, clearly. But Sammi wasn't upset. And maybe I was waiting for that cue. She'd said she couldn't drive, so I knew she was in shock and acknowledged that. But I didn't feel departed yet. Even a little bit. I felt very much alive. As far as I knew, I finished having sex with my girlfriend when I heard the screaming. The people at all the picture spots around the mountain had seen something horrifying. I had felt bad for them until I tried to pull Sammi close and my arms went through her. Then I felt bad for me. Actually, there was a period of time between pumpin' and a humpin' that I sort of blacked out. It was missing somehow. Like the file didn't save properly.

The first few minutes I was a ghost, my only concern was keeping Sammi calm. That was my goal. We were on the edge of the cliff having mind-blowing makeup sex

that was swirled in with the adrenaline boost we got from being so close to the edge. I was stupid. I mean, if I was really dead.

Sammi was passed out now, her full lips slack. I forgot how beautiful she was like this. In repose when she wasn't up and fighting me. She looked like a vintage movie star with a Cupid's bow mouth and porcelain skin. If I was really, really dead, what scared me the most was that I would disappear before I could tell her that the fights didn't matter. It was the quiet that mattered. Her beautiful face and boundless adventurism. If we hadn't gotten into that stupid fight, there wouldn't have been makeup sex and I wouldn't have been launched off the cliff. Now, I had no idea if I'd end up spending the afterlife as a semi-opaque fixture in her reality. With her, but never able to touch her. What a fucking buzzkill death was.

I sat up and was able to rest my back on the headboard. I just had to concentrate on the moment it happened a bit. The more I tried to focus, the more I realized I had some kind of memory block. My thoughts were, *sex, pussy, sex is the best, I love my dick, her pussy loves my dick, my dick loves her pussy, pound harder...* and then I could see through myself.

I didn't believe the cops when they said her pussy had shot me off the mountain like a cannon. She was good. Hell, she was amazing. There were times I thought she was writing her name in cursive on my dick through Kegel exercises during sex, but she couldn't launch me.

That was an insane conclusion to come to, but the cops couldn't see that I was a ghost standing right there.

I knew that now. And I needed to know more about this supernatural part of the world. I couldn't be the only dead dude hanging around in a semi-transparent state. I leaned down and gave her a ghost kiss on the forehead. She was supposed to be up at noon, and I knew the melatonin would keep her out like she'd been hit over the head with a mallet.

I needed to find out more. Maybe see my body. See what the hell was happening on the mountain, because something was seriously off up there.

I rolled out of bed and landed facedown on the floor, except it didn't hurt and the floor didn't completely stop my soundless fall. Instead, I found myself staring at old Ms. Pontoon's naked butt, her bedroom being right below ours. I was grateful that she required hearing aids, otherwise she would probably hate us. We fucked like we were trying to break the bedframe. And sometimes each other. We angry fucked a lot. The orgasms were out of this world. In fact, we'd had to replace our bedframe more than once in the two years we'd been living in this apartment. We'd also replaced the drywall behind our headboard. We'd dented it so many times, I actually put one of those cushioned memory boards up so I wouldn't have to keep patching the drywall. I sucked at that.

Ms. Pontoon rolled over and I got an eyeful of her hairy crotch muppet. Her mudflaps with nipples sprawled on the mattress on either side of her. I tried to do a push-up, but I seemed to be stuck halfway between my own floor and Ms. Pontoon's ceiling. It took me several minutes and a lot of concentration before I was finally able to roll over and pull myself back up to my apartment floor.

I lay there, huffing and puffing from exertion, until I remembered that I was dead and I didn't even need to breathe, let alone huff and puff for dramatic effect. I hopped to my feet, half-expecting Sammi to be awake and silent-laughing at me, but she was still passed out. I could see her nipples peaking the fabric of her jammies, which was one of my old t-shirts from college. It helped erase what I'd just seen in the bedroom below ours.

If I wasn't dead, I would have reached over and circled that nipple with my finger, but I was worried one of two things was going to happen if I did that: my finger would either go right through her body or she'd wake up and freak out over the ghost of her almost-fiancé touching her nipple. Either seems less than ideal.

I wandered through the apartment, no longer bashing my shin on the corner of the bed because I was no longer corporeal. I didn't accidentally bump into things. Instead, I went right through them. I stopped in front of the kitchen counter, where Sammi was forever leaving her keys. They were a foot away from the key rack I installed on the wall to make it easier for us to find them. I was the only one who used it. Also, by "installed," I actually meant that I used 3M tape to make it stick to the wall. Sammi didn't trust me with a drill. Or even a hammer.

I tried to pick up the keys, but my fingers kept going right through them. After two solid hours of trying, I was finally able to pick them up. I half-wanted to wave them around in victory, but I didn't want to lose my hold on them.

Before I left the apartment, I checked on Sammi one last time. Her lips were parted and she was snoring gently and doing that weird thing where she puffed out her breath on the exhale. I used to flick her ear until she stopped. But that was back when I could really touch her and not poke my finger through her. I sighed and left her in the bedroom. I needed answers, and she needed me to not be creepy and watch her sleep.

I got as far as the hallway. I could pass through the doorway, but the keys stayed inside the apartment.

"Fuck my life," I muttered as I stared at my empty hand and the door.

At the same time, the elevator doors across the hall slid open on a ding and our neighbors from down the hall stumbled out. They were forever at nightclubs and always three sheets to the wind. Lou-Ellen tripped over her own feet and plowed right through me before smacking her face on the wall.

"Ow! Shit."

"You a'ight?" Melvin, who usually smelled like a combination of cigarette smoke, old cheese, and body odor, mumbled.

Lou-Ellen recovered and I stepped out of the way to avoid being walked through again. It was a strange feeling. Not one I was particularly fond of.

"I'm fine. Let's go make Pop Tarts." Lou-Ellen shivered and rubbed her arms. "They need to cut the air-conditioning in here."

I watched them weave back and forth down the hall like bumper cars driven by toddlers until they disappeared inside their apartment. They were notorious for setting off the fire alarm because they constantly burned things with their toaster oven.

As much as I wanted to head back up to the mountain, I didn't want Sammi to wake up alone and think I'd disappeared and wasn't coming back. And I was also now aware of the problems the neighbors were likely to start with their stupid Pop Tarts.

I followed Lou-Ellen and Melvin down the hall. I wasn't quick enough, and they slammed the door in my face. I hated the feeling of walking through inanimate objects, but I sucked it up and did it anyway. I was prepared for the gag-worthy odor that always emanated from their apartment and was surprised when my senses weren't assaulted.

I took a deep, unnecessary breath and realized that despite the shit-sty I was standing in the middle of, I couldn't smell *anything*. Countless bongs littered their coffee table. The couch was the color of infant poop and still managed to have enough stains on it that it appeared as though it had a rainbow pattern.

I could've sworn I smelled Sammi's face wash when she'd been in the bathroom earlier tonight, but maybe I could only smell her, much like she was the only one who could hear and see me. It was another question to add to the list.

My time in Lou-Ellen and Melvin's apartment was blissfully short. They had one of those toasters with a cancel button. As soon as they left the room, I started trying to push the button. I mastered the skill before the

Pop Tarts could burn and wake up the entire building. I was pretty grateful that I couldn't smell the Pop Tarts. I fucking loved those damn things. Especially the s'mores variety.

They were both passed out on the couch when I walked through the living room, mouths hanging open. Thankfully, there were no lit cigarettes to contend with. I wasn't sure I had the patience to try to pick up a lit cigarette and not butt it out on their arm.

I headed back to my apartment to tackle the key situation. It took me another half hour to manage that task again. I was grateful the living room window was cracked open. Sammi always wanted a little fresh air, and since we were up on the seventh floor, I didn't think it was much of an issue to keep the window open a few inches.

I tossed the keys into the alley between our apartment and the next one. They landed on the ground and not in the garbage dumpster, which was a serious bonus.

I was pretty sure I couldn't die again, so I debated jumping from the window like I was Spiderman. But the idea of going through the pavement like I did the floor when I rolled off the bed was less than appealing, so I took the stairs instead.

My keys were still where they landed by the time I made it to the alley. And while they didn't wind up in the dumpster, they did land in a puddle of nasty looking water. Thankfully, I couldn't smell it. I spent the next fifteen minutes trying to pick them up again.

At least it wasn't taking quite so long anymore. Maybe I was getting the hang of this ghosting thing. My Positive

Pete mood took a swan dive as soon I sat my ass down in the driver's seat, and once again, my keys ended up outside, on the ground.

And it only got worse from there, because before I could pick them up, a couple of dudes came out of nowhere and snatched them off the ground.

"Hey, man! Give those back!" I shouted, forgetting that no one could see or hear me, except Sammi who was still sleeping peacefully in our bed.

"Hey, man! Give those back!" one of the hoodie-wearing dudes screech-mocked me.

My voice was not high-pitched. It was deep and manly.

The other dude cackled along with him. "Look at this loser. Can't even pick up his keys."

They threw their heads back and guffawed loudly.

I was annoyed, but also suddenly hopeful because these guys, who were jerks, could apparently hear me. I got out of the car.

"Wait, you can hear me?"

"Can you hear me?" the same one who had mocked me the first time said again. He tugged his hood back and I made a face when I saw his face. Oh, these guys were clearly not alive anymore.

He had a giant black hole where his left eye should be. Brain matter was exposed, and it looked like a mass of raw meat and jagged bone. At least *my* face was still intact. His buddy dropped his hood, too, and I resisted the urge to run away. Running was not a manly ghost thing to do, but the dude had a slash across his neck that very much made it seem like his head was going to tip off his neck, especially

considering all of his villainous cackling.

I hated horror movies, and Sammi loved them. The gorier the better. I tolerated them because usually I could get her to give me a handy, or just sit in my lap and ride me reverse cowgirl while she watched them, but they gave me horrible nightmares.

And these two looked exactly like something from one of her scary movies. And they were apparently undead, like me. But they were . . . less see-through. Like real humans. But not alive.

"Stupid fucking newbies," Neck Gash cackled.

They pushed each other back and forth, laughing when one of them would go transparent and pop back up ten feet away. One-Eyed Brains dude disappeared. I glanced around the parking lot, searching for him.

Then I felt a tap on my shoulder.

In every single horror movie I'd ever watched, I'd spent an inordinate amount of time being angry at the stupidity of people. Never turn around when someone taps your shoulder in a dark parking lot being haunted by ghosts. And yet, like a horror movie idiot, I turned.

"Boo," One-Eyed Brains said not two inches from my face.

I was embarrassed by the bloodcurdling scream that ripped out of me. I slapped my hand over my mouth and glanced briefly in the direction of my seventh floor window. Then I realized I could lead these goons to my sleeping girlfriend and I had no idea what they were capable of, apart from being juvenile assholes.

If I'd been able to pee my pants, I was certain I would

have.

They started cackling again and calling me a loser as One-Eyed Brains hit the unlock button on my key fob and Neck Gash made a show of opening the passenger side door. He dropped in the seat and picked up one of the candies in the cup holder. It crinkled, and then he popped it into his mouth while One-Eyed Brains hopped into the driver's seat. He even adjusted the seat.

And rolled down the window. I had so many questions. Like, how the hell did they do that?

"Later, loser!" Neck Gash stuck his head out the window as One-Eyed Brains revved the engine and hit the gas. Neck Gash's head flopped over, exposing his severed spine before the car disappeared around the corner with a squeal.

"I can't believe I'm fucking dead and I've just been bullied." I kicked a rock, but, of course, my foot went right through it.

"Arrr, rough night, me boy…"

I stumbled back a step and landed inside someone's souped-up SUV. I peeked through the tinted window.

Sitting on the tailgate of the pickup beside me was a fucking pirate. He looked like he was right out of *Pirates of the Caribbean*. But thankfully, not decaying.

This night could not get any weirder.

Three

SPOILER ALERT: IT got weirder. I was looking at Johnny Depp's dead doppelgänger when he disappeared briefly then returned, easing my car back to my spot. The creepy ghosts were gone. I forced myself out of the SUV as he got out of the car like a normal human and even closed the door. He tossed me my keys, which went straight through my hand.

"Oh. You're new. So, so new. We call this the ghostymoon. When you aren't even lamenting and moaning yet." The pirate hooked his thumbs into his belt loops and rocked back on his for-real pirate boots.

"Moaning?" I stared at my keys on the asphalt. Not this again.

"Oh yeah, the ghost moans. They come from yer balls. Yer nethers." The pirate started a small shimmy in his shoulders that continued the length of his body until he got to his hips. A tiny echo of chains rattling emanated from

his crotch. Then I heard a noise that I'd heard before in my life. I remembered it, though I couldn't place it.

Groannnn. Moannnnn. Awwooooooo.

The pirate stopped his dance, and the night stilled with him. "Heard that in all yer nightmares, eh?"

And he was right. That's right where it had lived up until this moment. It was the soundtrack for the deep sleep where I'd run and not move, punch, and not connect. I was dumbfounded.

"That was you? With your musical balls?" I tried to look harder at his face, see if I could remember him from somewhere. "Who are you?"

"I'm Sharkbait McBeard." He flashed me a smile that was more gold than white. "You've heard of me, I'm bettin'. And all ghosts can do the moaning. Ladies do it with their buoys." He pointed at his chest. "Or their love canal." He pointed to his clanking balls. "But mostly that sounds like ghost farts. Anyway, as I said, me name's Sharkbait McBeard."

"The name rings a bell." The name did not ring a bell. I just didn't want to piss off any more ghosts that could drive a car.

"Ya can call me Shark." Shark took a deep breath and things inside him rattled around.

I tried the same move, and like before, I didn't need to. Nothing made noise inside of me.

"Look at that. Tight as a clam's ass. All yer parts and pieces are still pretending to be in yer body. 'Tis a sweet time fer sure." Shark stepped closer to me. "Ya can do less but feel more right now. How'd ya die? I don't see any

wounds on ya."

He was right. At least from the neck down, I seemed perfectly fine. I thought of the carjacking ghosts and shivered. I knew how they died from looking at them.

"I'm currently… well, my body is off the cliff at Lover's Peak. My girlfriend Sammi and I were, um, indisposed, and somehow I fell off. I mean, I was a ghost pretty much right away." I put my hand through my ghost hair.

"Oh sheet. Lover's Peak, ya say? Well, if yer were knockin' boots with yer lady friend, then you probably stirred up ol' Morven. He hates love. Especially on Lover's Peak. I'm betting he threw you off. Did Sammi die, too?" Shark put his knuckles under his chin and leaned toward me.

"No. No, she's fine. She's upstairs." I pointed at our place. Our window.

"Hmm. This one's a real seagull's folly." Shark put his fists on his hips.

He was so overdramatic that I was kind of wondering if he was a real pirate or some cosplaying weirdo ghost.

"Morven won't stop until yer both ghosts. Just so you know."

Fear trickled like sharp, cold fingernails down my spine. I had a burst of adrenaline, or whatever sent dead people moving, and before I knew it, I was standing at the end of my bed, looking at a melatonined Sammi. She was fine, her chest moving up and down peacefully.

I looked to my left and Shark was there, head tilted, watching Sammi as well.

"Ah, ferk, she's a beauty. Bosom like the bow of a ship,

lips like a mermaid's vagina."

I moved so that I stood between Shark and her, all of a sudden wanting to afford her some privacy.

"Ya love her." He tipped his chin back and I saw compassion in his eyes.

I tried another of those useless deep breaths. "More than anything."

"'Splains why yer still here. Which is good. Because nothing that lovely should ever have to deal with Morven on their own." He pointed through my chest at Sammi.

Four

SAMMI

I WOKE UP slowly. The melatonin kicked me right in the butt. I stretched out my foot to touch Evan's leg. Whenever my feet had a chill, his hairy furnace calf had the remedy.

I kept foot-looking and toe-searching until I opened my eyes. He was there, no pillow. My eyesight was still blurry with sleep.

"Don't play games. I had a dream you were a ghost. Let me touch your leg. The cold only stings for a little while."

Evan had often complained in the past about how shocking my ice frigid feet were, but he usually held steady like a real man should.

"Morning, babe."

I focused a little harder when I noticed his frown that he was trying to force into a smile. It gave him the thinking Kermit look.

He was see-through-ish. Faded like a flag that had spent too many afternoons in the hot sun.

"Yeah. I wish it were a dream, but it's an actual nightmare." Evan propped himself up on his elbow. "Meet Sharkbait McBeardy… he's also a ghost."

Evan looked toward the end of our bed. I turned my head slowly. I saw nothing except our serene gray and yellow furnishings.

"Maybe I'm still asleep and this is the melatonin doing me a dirty?" I pulled myself to a sitting position. The action caused a small fart to slip out.

"Oh! She's a feisty one. Filled with the morning fireworks! A good man knocks the farts outta his lass in the morning with a stiff boning."

And that's when I screamed for the first time today.

Evan surged quickly near me, too quickly. Less human than he had been last night. Which I knew in my heart had really happened, but seeing Evan as a ghost in the harsh light of day was tough. I wanted to be hugged, and he couldn't really accomplish that. Instead, his face was too close to mine as his arms encircled me in an embrace that held no comfort because I couldn't feel it.

He whisper-talked in my ear, "That's another ghost. He's helping me."

"There are other ghosts?"

The voice from the end of the bed gave a loud guffaw. "So ferking many ghosts that the planet is lousy with them! Aye, tell ya what, you've never pooped alone, if you know what I be sayin'."

I turned my head so I could look at Evan's face. "Did you have to fall off the cliff? If you had just kept your balance instead of trying to do the ice cream swirl, you'd

still be here. All the way."

I saw disappointment in his face. "You always love the swirl when you're orgasming."

"Well, you died. Is me getting the best O the priority?"

Evan and the ghost voice said, "Yes," at the exact same time.

"Men. Even dead men." I looked at my hands in my lap. "I have a list of things in my to-do box today. One of them is going back to the mountain to see if they can recover your body."

"Aye, wench. You better hope they can't reach his body, because if they get it, then his ghost is headed for the great horizon. And Morven wants you dead."

I held my hands up toward the sound of the voice. "Is this the Grim Reaper?"

"No. This is Sharkbait McBeard. He's a pirate. I was carjacked last night by two other ghosts. I like to think that their names are One-Eyed Brains and Neck Gash, or at least should be, but I'll spare you the details." Evan leaned back against our headboard and held. He didn't go straight through.

"I think the details are right there in their names." He was getting my frustration up, which had the side effect of getting my lady parts interested in his man parts.

I gazed around the bedroom and offered, "Thanks, Mr. McBeard, for saving Evan, I guess."

"Anything I can do to help a healthy lassie like yourself. I'm going to go over to Lover's Peak and see if I can keep yer body where it is."

I felt a whoosh like an air-conditioner had flicked on

and then watched Evan's shoulders relax a bit. He and his goddamn shoulders.

"Are there any more ghosts here?" I squinted to see if I could make any out. It seemed pointless since Mr. McBeard had just been a voice, but I wanted to make sure we were alone.

"Not right now." Evan was staring at me.

"What?"

The whole thing was unnerving. I was waiting to miss him. To cry over him. But he was right here with me like every morning.

"You want breakfast?"

I was hungry. "How are we going to manage that?"

Evan was an amazing cook. He would make me my favorite breakfast on mornings when we didn't have work. And today was Saturday.

"I've learned a few things overnight." He winked at me. I could still see the eyeball behind the lid while he did it.

"Okay, I can eat." I flipped the covers off only me.

Five

Evan

SSHARK HAD INDEED left. I wanted to Google both him and Morven to see if I came up with any information that would help. Sammi was still in denial. I mean, she hadn't cried yet. She was going to cry, right?

I tried to put myself in her shoes. I managed to crack the fridge enough to grab two eggs. The frying pan was harder, but I was starting to figure out that imagining the task you wanted to finish would expedite the process.

I got the burner on with two attempts.

As I went through the mundane act of cooking, I thought about the cops again. How they were afraid to approach her and were fascinated with her possible cannon pussy.

When I concentrated again, I was in the center of the police station holding my spatula.

I gasped, and then clamped my mouth shut, but no one reacted. Of course. I was a ghost. I was whooshing, or I had whooshed. Traveled like Shark.

"Pupperino case? Who's on that today?"

My last name caught my attention. The three cops from yesterday were huddled together. All at once they held their hands up in front of their chests like they were cuddling a set of large boobs. I recognized that fake cup size and placement. They were thinking about Sammi. All three of them.

"Michigan will go up and toss another tarp on the bod," the cop who had predominantly red ears yesterday offered up.

"I gotta couple of fresh ones in the trunk of my cruiser."

All three were still mimicking Sammi's boobs. A female cop walked by and smacked Michigan on the back of the head with a file folder. They all dropped their hands and mumbled *sorry* at her retreating form.

The captain ignored the whole scene and updated them, "Rescue said they would be out there at noon. But we all know how Lover's Peak goes, so make sure the tarping is accurate."

Michigan nodded once. "I'll take Corbey and Kackley with me to check on the scene. But all evidence and accounts point to a very unfortunate accident."

As soon as the captain disappeared and the female cop was gone, they all held their hands up like boobs again.

I thought of the actual boobs they were trying to imagine and wound up back in front of the oven looking at a naked from the waist up Sammi.

She was busy tossing flour onto the flaming pan of eggs. "You trying to kill me, too?"

She was furious.

All the blood in my body went rushing south. That was what happened whenever Sammi got pissed off, which honestly was often. And half the time I needled her just so we could angry screw. She tossed the frying pan onto the back burner where it sizzled and smoked and then she planted her hands on her hips.

"What in the actual hell, Evan? You can't just disappear in the middle of making breakfast. Where did you go?" Her voice was rising, sort of like one of those alarms that got louder and louder. When she reached the crescendo, we would always end up naked.

"Actually, since I'm a ghost, apparently I can just disappear in the middle of making breakfast."

Her nostrils flared. My dick punched at the front of my ghost pants. She threw the spatula at me, but instead of connecting with my crotch, it went straight through me and hit the hall where it left a dent in the drywall. It joined a small army of other dents. Some guys had marks on their headboards, I had flaws in the drywall.

"I can't even fight with you like this!" Sammi flailed her arms like a wonky windmill.

"I guess you'll have to try harder."

I imagined her running at me, which was exactly what she did, and instead of going through me, she collided with my half-opaque body. "What the…?"

I cupped her face in my palms. Two of my fingers disappeared into the side of her head for a second, but I was able to reposition them so they were in her hair, rather than inside her brain. Sammi tipped her head up, and I imagined the same scenario we'd repeated thousands of times over the years. Every time we fought it was the same dance.

She gripped my shoulders and her hands didn't go through me.

"Oh my God, Evan, I can touch you. How are you doing that? Never mind. I don't care." She latched onto the back of my neck and pulled my head down. I had to put all my energy and focus into what was going on when really my dick was screaming for attention.

I must have mumbled *shut up* out loud because Sammi bit my bottom lip. "Don't tell me to shut up. You shut up and kiss me."

I managed to get in a couple solid swipes of tongue and an ass grab before she fell through my body and landed on the floor.

"You did that on purpose!" Sammi rolled over onto her back and glared at me. The fire in her eyes stoked the fire in my loins. My dick wanted out of my pants and into my girlfriend.

"I didn't do it on purpose. I'm new at this ghost crap."

"You could make eggs no problem, but you can't even kiss me?"

Sammi had two modes, angry mode and tears mode, when it came to our fights. Angry mode was always the preferable of the two because it meant the sex was awesome. When we reached tears, sex was off the table. I needed to face the facts, I was just getting used to this ghosting business. There was a distinct possibility that I might not be able to follow through on sex, but damn, if I wasn't going to at least try.

"I think it's because you're touching me. It makes it hard to focus. If you just let me touch you, it might work better. Can you let me try something?" I dropped to my knees in front of her.

"Fine, but you better not go through my body again."

"I'll try not to." It was the best I could offer. There was a solid chance my less than solid body would go through hers again, but I would try my damnedest not to. I reached out and imagined cupping her boob. My palm curved around the swell without sinking right into her chest. "Fuck yeah," I muttered.

She gave me a look.

"What? Isn't this awesome?"

"Of course, you'd go for my boob first."

"Well yeah, it's always the starting point." I grabbed the hem of her shirt. In my excitement, my fingers went through it on the first try, but the second time around I got it.

Sammi raised her arms over her head and I managed to get the shirt off. Her bra wasn't quite as easy, so she took care of it for me and unleashed her glorious rack.

God, I loved her boobs. Almost as much as her pussy. Plus, there were two of them, one to fill each hand.

"Hello, ladies," I said to her boobs and then cupped them gently. With my attention fully occupied, I brushed my thumbs over her nipples and was rewarded with a soft gasp.

"You felt that?"

"Yeah, please do it again," Sammi asked.

If I wasn't semi-transparent, her hands would be in my

hair, yanking on it. But I didn't trust that I'd be able to keep my focus if she was touching me when I was touching her, so this was how it had to be.

She propped herself on her hands and leaned back into them, jutting her chest out. I moved in and sucked one of her nipples into my mouth. She moaned again, loudly. Once again, I was grateful that all of our neighbors were old and had terrible hearing, and that the air-conditioners sounded like jet planes landing in this building.

But when she pulled her signature move, gripped my hair and arched into my mouth, my face went through her body and I was suddenly looking at her hands on the floor behind her. I reared back, overcorrecting and slid backwards on the floor, my ass halfway into Ms. Pontoon's living room before I pulled myself back up to sit on the floor. "You can't do that!"

"I didn't do anything!"

"You can't touch me while I'm touching you. I need to fucking focus on your tits and you ripping my hair out by the roots is distracting."

"I was excited!"

"Just keep your damn hands to yourself. You know what? Take your pants off and lie down."

"Why should I if you're just going to keep yelling at me?"

"Because I'm going to try to give you an orgasm, that's why," I snapped back.

"Fine!" Sammi huffed and pulled her pants and underwear down. She tossed them through me and gave me her snooty face, but did what I asked and lay down on

the floor. I suppose she could've relocated to the couch, but we were here and I was determined to try to do this.

She spread her legs wide and exposed her pussy. She had a little tuft of hair at the top of her mound. I loved to pull on it when she yanked on my hair, just to piss her off. I would try that later. I slid back across the floor and knelt between her open thighs. Her clit peeked out at me from between her not-face lips.

I brushed over it with my fingertip and Sammi sighed.

"You should tuck your hands under your butt so you don't try to touch me again." I brushed over her lady bean again.

She grumbled, but complied.

I kept flicking her bean, doing the things she liked that got her all hot and excited. Sammi's hips started moving and her moans got louder and shriller. A dog howled from somewhere outside.

I tried the move where I slid two fingers inside and did the pumpity-pump while rubbing her orgasm button with my palm. Unfortunately, I couldn't account for all her flailing, so half the time my palm would go right through her pussy. My hand was probably in her uterus about fifty percent of the time.

"This is not deep enough! Go harder!" Sammi half-shouted.

Normally, this would be the point where she'd be grabbing onto my shoulders, biting them—she did that a lot—while she told me that I better make her come or she would never blow me again and I would tell her if she kept it up I was going to go anal on her with no lube. I would never actually do that. Anal always required lube, but that would often be enough to push her over the edge.

But all the hip thrusts and my not really being used to my ghost body made it impossible. It was ridiculously frustrating. I'd been making Sammi come on pretty much a daily basis for the past two years. It was damn well muscle memory and I wanted to make it happen.

Because I had no idea if I would ever be able to make it happen again.

Which was when I realized if I couldn't make her come I would never be able to have sex with her again. I unbuckled my pants and my erection sprang free. I gripped it in my fist. It felt real and usable. I removed my fingers, and Sammi's head, which had been thrown back in frustration while she fought for an orgasm that was just out of reach, suddenly snapped up.

I slapped her clit with my dick and almost did a touchdown dance when it didn't go right through her.

"Oh my God, get Thor in me."

Sammi always refered to my penis as though it was one of the Marvel superheroes. I liked Thor, so I didn't mind.

"You have to stay still," I reminded her.

"Okay, okay, I can do that." She splayed her legs out in a rigid V and balled her hands into fists.

I managed to line things up, imagining how warm and wet and tight it would be. I tried to keep my focus, but even with Sammi not touching me it was a lot of pressure. I was just about to try to get inside her without going through her when Sammi's phone rang.

Snapping my attention to the electronic device sent me

to her purse. My giant hard-on pointed at the noise the ringtone was making like a hunting dog that had found its target.

I looked over my shoulder to see my girlfriend's eyes narrow and her legs go limp. "Really?"

I looked down at my dick and said the same thing to him. He still pointed at Sammi's purse like it was his most important job ever.

By the time I got back to the kitchen, Sammi was up and swinging her naked ass toward the bedroom. "I have to go to the mountain. And stop for food. See if you can ghost clean this up, please."

I sighed and looked at the kitchen. Being a ghost sucked.

Six

EVAN

SAMMI DROVE SLOWLY. It was what she did. She stopped the car with plenty of room between her and the car in front of her. She slowed down at every intersection, even though I told her one day she would get rear-ended for doing just that.

At the last red light before the turnoff to the Lover's Peak parking lot, she looked over at me.

"I'm scared that you're going to leave."

The almost sex had tapped into her empathy. Her emotions. Maybe thundered through her shock a little.

"I'm right here," I stated the obvious.

She reached out her hand and it went through my thigh. We both stared at her hand touching the upholstery of her car.

The light turned green and she went back to the task of driving. Maybe we were both in shock. It's not easy to die. Harder to be a ghost. With the cops thinking about her 

boob size and ghosts lurking all around her, I was getting scared that I might leave, too. Even if it was the very last thing I wanted to happen.

I reached over and put my hand on her thigh, making a point to squeeze it gently. To reassure her, even though I had no idea what the future held.

SAMMI

I WAS A quiet walker. I snuck up on Evan all the time by mistake because of my light footfalls. Hiking up the trail to Evan's body with Evan's ghost was very silent. Ghosts had even softer feet than I did.

He was quiet with his mouth, too. I think we both had trepidation about confronting the reality of his corpse.

As I came upon the scene of our deadly sex, I could overhear the cops talking. It

seemed to be the same three from last night.

"Well, I don't know how you missed it last night in the dark, but you did."

"I didn't even see the nest. Can birds build them overnight? I mean, there's got to be a baker's dozen in there." Michigan was on his hands and knees, looking over the ledge.

I cleared my throat. The cops turned toward me.

"Hello, ma'am. Arrive here okay?" I finally had the sense about me to read his name above his pocket. Corbey.

"What's going on?"

Michigan had a stack of blue tarps next to his knees. Corbey with the red ears came to stand next to me.

"Well, your boyfriend had the unfortunate luck of landing right near an endangered species bird's nest. There are only twenty known examples of this branch of bird-dom here in North America." Corbey couldn't hold back a grin. "I love birds."

The pants adjusting cop with the pocket name of Kackley patted Michigan on the back and then headed over.

"We had to call a wildlife rescue to advise us how to proceed. All we've found was the penalty for injuring the bird or disturbing a nest—and it was pretty steep. Turns out, these birds have such a unique bird call, scientists are very interested."

"Fuck you!"

Michigan stood up. "The momma bird didn't like it, but that body is double tarped."

"Festering asshole!"

I looked from Evan to the cops, knowing my eyes were owl wide. "Is there an old woman down there?" I pointed to the cliff.

"Shitbag!"

"Oh no. That down there is a Foul-Mouthed Mountain Digit. They are one of the few birds that has vocal abilities and a very pronounced middle claw. Their beaks are turned just so they can hit the 's' sound in the alphabet."

I had to see it. I was compelled to see it. The bird sounded so human.

I inched closer to the edge. Michigan helpfully held out an elbow. I took it, even though I was pretty skilled at hiking. There was something terrifying about seeing the bird that made this shrewish noise.

I peered over. The first thing I noticed was the blue tarp with lumps underneath it. I had to look at Evan to be sure I still saw the ghost version of him. I did. He was leaning over with me.

Then I saw the bird swivel its head. It looked like the hairy old witch from *Sleeping Beauty*. And, hand to heaven, it gave me the middle claw while looking me dead in the eyes.

"Fuck you!"

"Oh my gosh." I gawked at Michigan.

"Right? That oversized chicken enunciates better than some speech pathologists I've met." He had a fondness on his face that was usually reserved for children taking their first steps.

"Turnip dick!"

Kackley was right behind me. "Honestly, the creativity and diction is just fascinating."

I studied it again. The bird had dingy feathers hanging around its face that looked like unwashed hair. It was hunched over its nest where putrid green eggs peeked out from around its fat bottom.

The bird went from giving me the finger to pointing it at Evan's body.

"Shart toolbag!"

It was like an evil wizard casting a spell.

I realized what I was looking at just before it happened. Evan's ghost was no longer next to me. He was standing on the thin ledge with his body. He ghost punched the foul-mouthed mother bird right in its horrible face.

Its head reeled back. I knew Evan could move stuff, but to get off that kind of a punch, he must have been really angry.

The bird extended its wings in response to the blow.

It screeched, "Boner dragon," at Evan while the cops tried to find the unseen attacker.

"Oh no." Just as Ghost Evan and the endangered bird started really going at it, another crew of four people arrived. They had *National Bird Rescue* written above the pocket of their khaki uniforms.

Evan settled into a fighting stance that I recognized from when we would hear weird noises in the middle of the night. This time, instead of the result being the furnace kicking on, he was for real throwing down.

Evan could be like this. He would bottle stuff up and then something would send him over the edge. Usually it was with me. Of course, instead of fighting with our hands, we fought with our genitals and liked it. A whole lot.

The bird got to its tiptoe claws, and I felt bad for it because it was ugly and, honestly, just trying to protect its inevitably ugly babies.

"Stop!" I hollered down the cliff. My voice echoed over and over. Evan peered up at me. He knew I loved animals. Even ugly cursing ones, apparently.

I watched as his shoulders dropped. He didn't want to fight anymore either.

The bird whipped its head around and snarled at me.

"Poison cooter!" It gave me the finger again. Well, the claw, but the sentiment was the same. I gave it the finger back.

Michigan put his hand on his chest. "It knows about your deadly pussy!"

The wildlife people were taking pictures and videoing. Evan looked from my face to the bird and gave it one last bitch slap before appearing next to me. He whispered in my ear, though he could've shouted. I was the only one who could hear him. "It's candy, baby. Not poison. Don't let that bird get you down."

The bird howled, "Tit fungus!"

"That bird reappeared to hark the end of times. We call that the Death Bird. Not a good omen."

The pirate voice again. I had to get out of here. Between the screaming curses and the ghosts, I was just not handling things anymore.

I spun on my heel and started the hike back down the mountain. Ghost Evan joined me. Once there was considerable distance between the cliff and me, I spouted off my frustration, "I guess your body is staying on the cliff tonight."

"You know, that's not necessarily a bad thing. I mean, according to Shark, I could disappear once my body does." Evan tried to hold a branch back from hitting me in the face. All he wound up doing was making it slap me harder.

"Seriously?" I held my hand up to my throbbing cheek.

"Oh, shit, I'm sorry. I just couldn't hold it back once it had tension. I'm sorry." He stepped in front of me and I stopped out of politeness and the true hate I had for the feeling I got deep down when we went through each other. He put his hands up on either side of my face and blew

gently on the skin that was stinging. His breath was cool and felt nice.

"It's not your fault you can't know how your ghost will interact with real stuff." I assessed his face. Was he softer now? Was he getting harder to see? I tried to distract myself from the worry that he was disappearing by bringing up Sharkbait. "So, the pirate ghost is still here. Where's his body? I mean, surely he's been dead a long time."

I saw Evan's head tilt before I heard the ghost we were talking about boom in my ear, " Aye, matey! She's a smart lass. Putting two and two together. Me body lies o'er the ocean."

I rolled my eyes. "This bullshit right here…"

"Hey, Shark, this is sort of a rough time for us. Maybe back up, like, at least twelve inches and give us some privacy." Evan put his arm around me. I tried to thread my fingers through his and failed. Instead, I just twisted my head so I could look at his face.

"If ye really wanna know, my body is actually over the ocean, in a museum. About pirates. So, I'm here for a while."

Evan just stared down at the spot that had been talking.

"Okay. I'll get ta looking for ol' Morven. You kids get to fighting or whatever you like to do best."

Evan looked down at me. "He's gone. And we can leave, too. Get home."

Well, at least we agreed on that.

Seven

EVAN

I CONCURRED WITH Sammi that she deserved a little alone time in the apartment. She chose our main bedroom suite with the attached bathroom. I sat at the kitchen table with my iPad. If I could really focus, I could get some reaction from the touch screen. It took way more energy than it ever did in life, but I was able to do an internet search to try to compile knowledge about what Sammi would be facing.

The results for Sharkbait McBeard led nowhere. If he was a famous pirate, no one else knew about it but him.

Now, Morven was another story entirely. There was regional lore about his ghost that seemed to even be accompanied by a cult-like following. Sightings were usually around Halloween and at night. He was either eight feet tall with giant teeth or a deadly guy with knives for elbows and no eyeballs. None of the illustrations people had cobbled together were inspiring any kind of

reassurance that Shark was wrong about the guy.

Next, I looked up Lover's Peak. What caught my attention was the Halloween time accidents on the mountain. People falling down the cliff. Most lived, but a few died, most recently me.

I felt Sammi come into the room, the air moving me a bit. She couldn't sneak up on me anymore.

"How's it going? Do we really have to worry about Morven?" She leaned her hip against the table while she scanned the screen of information. I tapped the home screen to close it down. I didn't want to scare her unnecessarily.

"I can't tell." I was lying, but for her to tell that when I had been alive she'd rest her fingers on my throat. If my heartbeat was fast, she'd say I was fibbing. And she was almost always right. Unless she was wearing a low-cut blouse.

This time all she could do was whisper-touch the skin on my neck. No heartbeat to judge.

"I kind of want to go back up to the mountain and just... dare him to touch me. Scream at the top of my lungs." She fisted her hands into unthrown punches.

"I need to know how to protect you—if he *is* real. I won't watch what happened to me happen to you." I stood in front of her, touching her fists.

The stages of loss were coming. I think she was edging off of denial and into anger.

"You can't stop me." She lifted her chin. In the world of the living, just putting my massive body in her way was enough to dissuade her from flying out of the apartment in anger.

"No, I can't. You're right. And we usually handle a lot of our decisions with regret because we don't think things through." I touched her hair, still able to move it out of her eyes.

She looked at our feet. "You're right about that."

"Then let's get prepared to fight this. Let me talk to Shark again—get him to train me on what I can possibly do and what you can do. I'll invite him here." I leaned down and kissed her forehead.

"He creeps me out. I mean, he's only a voice. At least I can *see* you." She went to her tiptoes and pursed her lips. I gave her the kiss she was asking for.

"I think it's totally okay if ghosts creep you out." Was she always this beautiful? Why did I fight with her so much when I was alive?

"I think that's fair, for sure. Just don't leave me alone with him."

"I won't. I won't leave you until someone forces me to." I was really glad she couldn't tell I was lying this time, too. I had no idea how much time I had left and when I would be forced to move on to the next life.

SHARKBAIT STOOD IN front of me, gold teeth gleaming. "Sorry, I'm so happy. I know your corpse is still not even in the ground. But I just saw my love."

Sammi edged into the living room from the bedroom. Clearly, hearing about Shark's romance had piqued her interest.

"How can one be so comely? My sweet dimpled bottom. I love me my mermaid so much." He clutched his chest and the jewelry he was wearing clanked.

While I watched Sharkbait, the little specks of dust that usually floated in sunlight avoided him. As he started to talk about the mermaid's lovely scales, I zoomed into the kitchen. I was able to hold a small handful of flour from the ever-open bag in the pantry. I zoomed back into the living room and tossed the handful at Sharkbait. The flour dusted him. He stopped mid-guffaw and gave me an insulting staredown.

"What ye hell?"

"I can see him! Sort of!" Sammi squinted and approached.

She stuck out one finger and jabbed at Shark's arm. Her finger went through it, but there was sort of a hint of where Shark was. I was rewarded with a full smile from Sammi.

Where my heart used to be stung, she made it hurt. The thought of losing that smile to the ether or wherever the hell I landed after this world made me want to cry.

"So, Shark, what's Morven's deal? Am I really in danger?" Sammi leaned toward the ghost. Seeing him clearly helped her deal with her fear of him. Disembodied voices *were* pretty scary.

Sharkbait put one foot up on our coffee table and propped an elbow on his knee, like he was posing for a brand of rum. "Ah. Morven is a spirit as old as me, maybe older. He finds places that give people joy and tries to ruin 'em. Word has it that he's never had an epic love in his ever-lovin' life." Sharkbait scratched his voluminous

beard.

"So, he kind of sounds like a little bitch?" Sammi observed.

Shark's eyes went wide as he quickly put a floury index finger to his lips. He hissed around his finger, "Don't ya be taunting him, lassie. He might hear ya."

Sammi moved closer to me. "Well, does he do anything that we could say *nice* things about?"

I put my arm around her lower back and kept my hand on her hip. My feisty Sammi. She'd rather fight than show fear, and I loved that about her right now.

"I'm sure he was a fine looking man in his time." Shark started looking around the apartment like he was afraid of Morven popping up right away.

"What can a ghost do to me? Boo all night?"

I looked down at her long eyelashes as I murmured, "Well, he did kill me so…"

She tipped her head up toward mine and I saw sadness creep over her face.

Sharkbait cleared his throat. "Lassie, I appreciate all yer get-up-and-go, but we can only do so much from our side. Ya have to take care a yerself."

Sammi shrugged. "When it's your time, it's your time. If this thing wants me dead and no one can stop it, then I'm going out in a blaze of glory. Screw him. I will not lose the love of my life and gain fear of everything else in the same week."

Love of my life echoed in my head. We hadn't said it in so long. The big L word. Sure, when we were first together and seeing stars every time we orgasamed, we said it. But as time moved on and we had fallen into a routine, we didn't see the need for saying *love* every other sentence. It had slipped through the cracks, not making it into conversation at all anymore. But now, with her life in danger from God knows what and my body and me not being in the same place, I'd give anything to tell her over and over how much I was in love with her. And I wasn't wasting any more time.

I stepped between Shark and Sammi. "Hey, I love you. You were the love of my life, too."

This moment should've been about so much happiness. Instead, it was dripping with bittersweetness.

"Aye! That's beautiful. And so ferking sad. Crackers on Christmas. I want to just cry so hard my mermaid love could swim in me tears. Let me give you a few tips, Sammi. You know how ya boyfriend tossed flour on me for you to see me? That werks a lot of the time. Best during the day, when the sun is high in the sky. But yer can make it work when the moon is straddling us all, too."

"So, how can I stop him? Or redirect him?" Sammi folded her arms.

"Well, he loves bosoms." Sharkbait shrugged.

"How can boobs stop him?" Sammi covered her chest.

"Well, just seeing them stuns a guy. Any guy, dead or alive." Sharkbait rocked back on his heels.

"That's more a psychological observation than a ghost tip," I pointed out.

"True as yer ass points to the ground, Evan." Shark put his thumb to his bottom lip and tapped. "Fear helps a ghost that's got a bad way about 'em. So speakin' yer

mind and being brave? That will dull his powers against ya, fer sure."

Sammi didn't seem very assured by the vague instructions. "Awesome. So I hope him to death?"

"Well, ya be hoping him to life, not death. That's all I've got to offer. Now, I want to go back to me mermaid and see if she likes this flour ya tossed on me. Maybe she'll lick it off me." Shark went into our kitchen and skillfully opened the refrigerator door. "Oh, lookie that! Ya got one of these fancy bouquets me mermaid devours!" He held up a head of green leaf lettuce. "Ya mind if I bring it with me? Just fer her?"

"Have at it." Sammi waved a hand to give him permission. When Shark opened the door, we observed the head of lettuce going out into the hall.

Sammi and I spent the rest of the day in bed, researching ghosts and old folklore about what happened to spirits after they left their bodies. We went down some very strange Wikipedia rabbit holes. Ghosts, for sure, existed— we knew that from the last forty-eight hours. But when exactly they were forced to leave this terrestrial plane was another thing entirely.

Eventually, after a quick meal for Sammi that did not include a salad, we found a local social media post mentioning a police force member who had a side gig as a psychic. Both Sammi and I recognized him once we scrolled to the picture. It was Michigan, the tarp throwing champion cop.

"Things are getting even fishier than before. Fishier than even Shark's mermaid, who I am having suspicions might be a manatee." Sammi reached for her bottle of melatonin gummies. "I have to knock myself out. But tomorrow when we go check on your body, I'm talking to Michigan."

She leaned forward and gave me a kiss. Then she gently wiped some residual flour off of my ghost cheek. "Maybe I have to dust you with some flour, too. Like a breaded piece of chicken."

"I'll be your parmigiana." I watched her settle in for the night. How had I ever watched TV instead of staring at her? Now that time was so, so scarce, I realized how much of it I had wasted. And I didn't want to leave. I counted the deep breaths she took to pass the time while she got her human rest.

Eight

I WOKE UP knowing Evan was a ghost this time. My melatonin dreams were centered around losing him. There were also a clown and a giant fan and that cursing bird, but waking up knowing your boyfriend was dead sucked. I opened my eyes and breathed a sigh of relief. He was still here. See-through, but smiling.

"Morning, gorgeous." The dimples. The white smile.

In real life he woke up grumpy and would actively only speak to me using his middle fingers as directional signals.

"You waking up friendly now?" I turned to my side and missed him while staring at him. I wanted to nestle into his chest and feel his heat. Feel his coarse chest hair on my cheek.

"I woke up stupid every day we dated."

"Um." I wasn't sure where this was headed. He looked... pensive. Regretful.

"I just spent seven hours counting your breaths. Because

at least I was able to be near you. To hear you. Sammi, you are the most genuine person. The way you leave out water on the balcony for that one pigeon that has a nest out there. The way you refuse to ever let a bottle stay in the trash when you can recycle it. The trick you do with your tongue when you're sucking my dick. All of it is a miracle. *You.* I wasted being with you all this time by fighting about stupid stuff. You can fight with me whenever you want. I'll never do anything but let you win anymore. You slay me. You're so fucking beautiful. And I'm petrified of having to spend eternity missing you. Because that would actually be hell."

He tried to touch my hand twice, and the image of his hand went straight through. I didn't even get the cold chill. Panic seized my heart. Maybe I didn't have time to figure this out. Maybe I would lose Evan.

"Shit." I tried to grab his hand and had the same result. "You should've woken me up. Why would you let yourself fade more and not wake me up?" I was getting mad now, letting anger take over from where the impending grief made me feel helpless.

"I didn't want to wake you. You'd had a big day." He wasn't fighting back.

"Don't you Ghandi smile at my ass like you're three steps from the pearly gates." I tried to snarl at him. Instead, I snorted and had to blow my nose.

"Let's make a plan for today." He smiled again, letting my jab fall away like a leaf in autumn.

I liked plans. They kept me focused. And grounded. And happy. Evan was trying to keep me happy.

Why was he being the perfect guy when he was dead?

"Sounds good. I have Michigan's business card. I'll send him a text about your body and today's recovery mission."

Officer, this is Sammi from Lover's Peak. Curious if you need me up there when you remove my boyfriend's body from the endangered bird's cliff today? Thanks.

A message buzzed back quickly.

Miss Riggs, we will be up at the mountain today, but you can wait for my phone call or text later. We arc having a few emergencies up here on Lover's Peak, so it's best if you stay off the scene today.

Evan was pacing now. "Well, that doesn't sound good at freaking all. Maybe look at the local police Twitter and see if there's been activity or something?" He ran a hand through his ghost hair.

It was a good idea. I held my phone and hesitated.

"What? What's wrong?" He stood close to me and looked at the black screen.

"I don't want to go to their site. I know it'll have information about your accident there, and I just don't want to see it in black and white, you know? Does that make sense?" I sat down on the edge of the bed and let my phone lay in my lap.

Evan's left eye started to twitch, an indication that we would fight soon. Even my nipples got hard seeing his temper starting to flare. But then he swallowed whatever he was going to say. Like he actually swallowed it—I saw his Adam's apple move.

Instead, he offered, "Let's head back up the mountain.

Maybe we'll get lucky and I'll run into Morven and wring his neck myself."

I had doubts about that. He couldn't even give me the chills this morning. I liked the idea of going back to the scene. I was very interested to see what the hell Michigan was talking about. What could be an emergency when Evan was already dead? And honestly, until Evan's body was taken care of, I felt like I'd always be thinking of him up there. Feeling incomplete that I'd left our date with only part of him. And another hopeful part of me thought if we got his body back, we could somehow jam his soul back in there. Then everything could go back to normal again.

WE DIDN'T GET very far on the hike before we came up on our favorite three cops in riot gear.

"Hey. Um, I decided to come after all. What's going on?"

Corbey cleared his throat. "Well, Miss Riggs, the good news is the cursing bird's eggs have cracked and, well, the miracle of life is happening right there next to your dead boyfriend's body. It's amazing. The bird is utilizing Evan's body hair to fortify her nest. It's really tremendous to see."

I watched Michigan as Corbey prattled on about how cute the baby cursing birds were. He was looking from the spot where Evan's ghost was next to me and then back again. Michigan was aware of Evan. I would bet the house

on it.

Evan must have noticed the same thing, because he tested him by walking around in a big circle. Michigan paid just enough attention to Evan that I was really putting some credence to the information we found out on the internet last night.

Maybe Michigan could really talk to ghosts. Corbey's walkie-talkie burst forth with crackling white noise.

"The gang is on the move. Repeat, the gang is on the move. Make sure your jock straps are in place and you have a bushel of wineberries on hand."

The use of the word "gang" was interesting. I wasn't sure how much gang activity would be going on at the top of a hiking mountain. Then there was a deep chittering. The cops all found places to hide as I stood there looking for the source of the noise.

I couldn't see anything, but I could sense it. Something was coming. Michigan appeared at my side and whisper-yelled that I had to get the hell out of the open. He pushed me behind a large oak tree as the chattering was accompanied with the mass movement of branches.

Something huge was coming. Or a huge lot of somethings was coming. I watched as Michigan began whipping the wineberries around the tree as if they were ammunition. He had a jock strap pulled over the top of his SWAT pants.

"What is that?" Michigan had me pressed against the tree. Evan was trying to slide between us, but I ignored him.

Michigan's ice-blue eyes were intense. "The cursing

birds called forth the rabid raccoon packs. We should've seen this coming." He paused to toss a berry. "They get drunk off of these wineberries, and then we can get them loaded up into the wildlife preserve trucks. Our job is to make sure the coons don't breach the perimeter."

Michigan's ample tool belt was pressing against my stomach.

"Why the jockstraps?" I couldn't imagine why that was part of the protocol.

"They have human teeth and they go for the gonads. Straight for them. It's terrifying. Many a man has become a soprano because of the rabid raccoons' pack."

Michigan looked up and down my body. "You're obviously not in possession of a set of nuts, so you should be fine without a jockstrap."

"Can I get some berries?" It seemed like the only logical conclusion after he'd spewed his weird scenario.

"Sure thing." He held up a branch and I picked a few berries off.

Evan whispered in my ear, "Stay here with this guy. I'm going to see if I can find Morven. And raccoons can't bother me. I'm dead." He walked away a few steps before coming back to me.

I saw Michigan's jaw twitch and his neck get tense.

"And this guy wants to bone you. So don't let your boobs fall out or anything."

I gave Evan a harsh look.

Freaking ghost boyfriends.

Nine

EVAN

WELL, THAT GUY was going to ask Sammi out as soon as my body was gone. He was pulling her to him and pressing her against the tree like they were auditioning for a Hallmark movie. And she wasn't noticing. Hell, she hardly noticed anything at all when it came to guys hitting on her. I asked her three times to go get dinner before she finally clued in that I was interested in more than pork dumplings.

I was pulled in two directions: I wanted to handle Morven—however I would do that—and I wanted to stay close to Sammi.

After skirting a clump of oak trees, I saw the rabid raccoons. On a good day, I was always down for a trash panda. They're adorable and roly-poly. Adding the rabidness to their personalities was not a plus. The foaming lips and the snarling human looking teeth on this particular breed were definitely taking them right out of

the cute territory.

I could sense the other ghost before I saw him. He was much more of an old-timey ghost than I was. His clothes were in tatters, and his eye sockets were mostly hollowed out. He was busy scaring the raccoons from behind. When they would slow, he would hit them with pebbles and swish at their fat little butts with a branch.

"Go eat the girl. Get the girl. She's on my mountain."

"You own the mountain?" *Oh crap*.

He lifted his ghostly head and set those two black eyeholes in my direction.

"Die!" He flew at me, a million miles an hour. His face and body were a blur as his energy rushed toward mine. I flinched and cowered down. I had the very, very unpleasant experience of feeling another man's ghost nuts go right through my forehead.

And then I heard laughing. I covered my hairline and frowned. I wasn't sure why I had ducked. He couldn't really do anything to me, could he?

"Who owns the mountain? I do. The man who just put his gonads *through* your brain. I dipped my cobblers into your frontal lobe!"

He was still laughing. I was not impressed.

I stood. "So you're on this mountain, scaring sick raccoons? That's what your existence amounts to? I'd rather get steam-nutted by a delusional ghost than *be* the delusional ghost."

His frown was deep. "You. I know you. Your body is making a nest for my birds."

"Yeah, and you're the one that killed me, so I'm glad I

made an impact." I closed one eye as my bad pun floated between us. I tried to move the conversation around the awkward. "You said they're your birds? The cursing assholes?"

Again he moved in a flash and I had his skinny fingers digging into my neck. I could see he was trying to hurt me, but all I felt was a mild pressure, like a seatbelt. "You're going to have to try harder than that, you old geezer."

"I don't need to hurt you to destroy you, Evan. Your lady friend is here on my mountain. You might have dragged me down with you to your doom, but I have my eyes on her—so I *will* have her." Morven glowered at me.

"You don't even have any eyes." I folded my arms across my chest, slightly pushing them into his ghost form.

"You want to be a wise ass?" Morven grew bigger and bigger until he seemed to reach the clouds above. He was long and stretchy, like he was made of slime. His voice was deeper and seemed to vibrate the earth under my feet. "I will have her and anything she loves!" He opened up his huge arms.

"You better stock up on Yankee Candles and matte lip-gloss." I cupped my hands around my mouth and shouted, "Why do you have to be involved?"

And as soon as I asked, I knew. I remembered my death. I could taste it now. Morven's horrible face had appeared in front of me as I was hitting Sammi doggy style. I'd thought we were alone—I mean, I knew it was a public place and there was a chance of getting caught, but that usually made things hotter.

And then he'd raged. That deep voice I'd just heard

now—his ghost had emanated it then, too. He'd reached for Sammi and I caught him up. My love for her and my need to protect her felt like a superpower. My adrenaline soared through me as Morven had pushed me off the mountain using those same sound waves that he'd used now. It'd caused me to stumble on the pile of gravel near the edge. And he'd turned toward Sammi as I fell backwards. I think I was sitting in the limbo between life and death there. I was a little bit ghost and he wasn't as transparent as all the ghosts I had met since that moment. I was able to wrap my arms around him and drag him with me over the cliff.

I felt the second my body hit, and then I was tossed right back up next to Sammi. She could see me and talk to me.

Maybe it was because I had dragged Morven off the cliff and through her that I became a ghost so quickly?

"You remember how it was now? Do you understand why I need her dead yet?" He got smaller now, but his voice was still booming.

"I don't remember that part." I told him the truth.

I was just remembering the gory details of my fall, but I wasn't sure why he was so angry with me.

He put his nose close to mine, and those two sunken eyeballs became my own private movie screen. An old scene. This very ghost as a human—hell, he almost looked like he could be related to me and he was dancing with a woman. A woman whose shape I knew like the back of my hand. The movie showed him cradling Sammi's beautiful face, but she was in a pioneer-type dress.

"Before Samantha was yours, she was mine."

And then he flashed away.

SAMMI

MICHIGAN WAS A decent guy. He let me throw berries and filled me in on how a few times a year, the traveling band of rabid raccoons had to be fended off and rounded up. The cursing birds were apparently these raccoons' worst enemies, and they took offense to the foul language. I had no idea there were gang wars for wildlife, but it made sense. There were a lot of differences among them. There was a turn in the evening that sent the raccoons scrambling. Michigan reacted quickly and heaved me up toward the branches of the tree. I hadn't climbed a tree since I was a teenager, but some things stuck with a person and I was able to shimmy up a few feet. Michigan soon came after me, and we were facing opposing branches.

"Can't raccoons climb? Aren't they, like, super good at that?" Most of my exposure to raccoons were YouTube videos and they had little people paws. They were good at opening things and I figured climbing as well.

Michigan nodded solemnly. "Yes. Usually. But when they're rabid and there are ghosts around, they stick close to the ground unless cornered."

He resumed sweeping the area with his gaze. Then he unclipped a pair of what looked like sunglasses and slid them on. He tapped his temple. "Night vision."

That made sense. If it were night.

"They help me see the raccoons and pick up on any hints of ghosts." He swung his head back to me. "And something is stirring them up something awful right now."

Evan was next to me on my tree branch in a flash and I turned to face him. I didn't ask if he'd met Morven, because his expression told me everything. His lips were slack and his eyes were sad. His eyebrows seemed to be in a permanent up position.

Michigan spoke up, "Listen, I know you two are going through a tough time. I'll come to your place later and help you get hard. Just buy me a six pack of beer and a plate of brownies."

Corbey stomped into a clearing by our climbing tree. "Wildlife is done. The craziest thing. The raccoons ran into the truck. Didn't even need to corral them. It was like something scared the bejeezus outta them."

Corbey moved to the bottom of the tree and held up his hands. "I'll spot ya, miss. You just come on down."

Getting out of the tree was a little trickier than getting into it, but Michigan and Corbey helped from both ends.

When all three of us were on the ground, Kackley laid out the rest of the day. "Now that we're clear to head up, we can see if Michigan can assess the tarp situation on the body. Then we can see if rescue can get out here before night."

And that's when Corbey was hit on the top of the head by lightning.

Ten

EVAN

W HEN SAMMI AND I got back from the mountain meeting, she needed to shower immediately. I knew she was embarrassed that she'd peed her pants, but considering how everyone up there had done the same, I didn't think there needed to be shame about it at all.

The water cranked on and the pipes started to whine. Sharkbait was in front of me shaking his head.

"Yer survived a run-in with Morven. That's amazin'." He tucked both hands into the front of his pants. Deep. Too deep for company.

"How did you know?" It seemed like everyone on the mountain wanted to talk about anything but the otherworldly lightning.

"You know Brains and Gash? They werk fer me. They love the mountain when ol' Morven hits it with the bolts. They say they can feel something again. I gotta try it. But I was in deep with my mermaid love." His hands in the

front of his pants wiggled.

"The two ghosts that scared the shit out of me and jacked my car work for you?" I looked at the ceiling. Ridiculous.

"Of course! Imma pirate, matey. Not everyone has ships these days. So we take cars fer a joyride. They do take it a bit too far. Both the pranks and the cars." Sharkbait smiled like he was talking about misbehaving first graders instead of ghastly grown-ass man ghosts. "I needed a crew. Can't be a pirate without me crew." He shrugged. "So tell me what happened with the lightning."

Sharkbait sat down on the stepstool we had so Sammi could reach the top shelves in the kitchen.

I could hear that the water was still on, so I indulged him. "Well, Corbey, one of the cops handling my body up there, was talking to us, and then out of nowhere a giant bolt of lightning hit him on the top of the head."

"Aye. And then he pissed himself like he was chewing on a livewire, eh?" Shark leaned over and ghost farted, which annoyingly moved me twelve inches to the left. "And then what happened?"

I was getting the idea that Shark knew exactly what was happening in this scenario, but I kept going. "Well, Michigan, another cop, recognized the lightning as the Urine Bolts. Told us that Lover's Peak has unexplained lightning storms that are isolated to the top of that particular mountain, and before he could bring up his weather app…"

Shark filled in the not-so surprise ending, "He got slapped with a bolt and pissed his pants."

"Yeah. And then, the storm intensified and anyone who was on the mountain was getting hit. As they tried to get down the mountain, one after another was repeatedly hit. It was like watching a choreographed dance. Zap, piss, dance, walk, zap, piss, dance." I mean, it was clear that it wasn't fatal, thank heavens, and in hindsight it was kind of hilarious. I bit both sides of my smile.

Shark didn't bother hiding his. "Ferking Morven. He's evil, but he does have a flair for comedy."

I was too busy laughing at the image of the cops and Sammi dancing down the mountain to notice that the water had turned off. My first hint that she was done was when she was standing in the kitchen clutching a towel to her bosom. I wanted to apologize for laughing, but I was in too deep. Shark took one look at her angry face and he flashed out of the kitchen to somewhere else entirely.

"Evan, if you're laughing about me pissing my pants, I'm going to…" Before she finished, she started laughing with me instead of getting mad.

She tried to add some of her observations, but she could only get out a word or two before waving her hand in front of her face and gasping for air.

The doorbell rang and she took a moment to compose herself. She used the edge of her towel to wipe the tears from her eyes. I got a great glimpse of all of her beautiful, naked curves before she smoothed out the terry cloth and headed for the door.

She swung it open while holding the towel and I watched as Michigan's jaw dropped.

"I apologize. I had to shower. And I assumed you did,

too?" Sammi pointed at Michigan's jeans.

He was out of uniform now and holding a six pack of beer and a plate of brownies, which was good since I'd forgotten that he'd requested them. "Oh yes. Every time that happens, we all have to shower up. I was able to grab one at the station and stop off to get what I needed to make your boyfriend hard."

There was that terminology again that had befuddled me the last time. Before the errant, non-deadly lightning storm.

I was not looking for this dude to get me hard, but Sammi held open the door and invited him in.

Eleven

Evan

MICHIGAN CAME PREPARED. I was in the perfect mood to eat brownies and have a beer. If I was alive.

Sammi offered, "Pardon me while I get into some actual clothes. Can you see Evan? Is that what you said?"

Michigan closed the door behind him with his foot and juggled the things he was carrying so he could shake my hand.

He obviously was just going through the motions, because I couldn't grab him and vice versa. "I'm Flint Mistro. From Michigan, hence the nickname that's stuck."

I pretended to shake his hand as Sammi slipped back into the bedroom.

"I can't hear you, if you have anything to say, but I can see you. So before she gets back, did she have anything to do with your death that I haven't been able to detect?"

I shook my head no.

"Good. Good to hear. I had a feeling it was just Lover's

Peak being Lover's Peak, ya know." He moved into the kitchen and set down the beer and brownies. After taking out two cans, he put the rest in the fridge like he lived here.

Sammi returned in jeans and my old college sweatshirt, her wet hair up in a clip. And, of course, a little lip-gloss.

"Hi. Were you talking to Evan?" She stood close to Michigan and squinted in my direction.

"I can talk to him, but he can't talk to me. The reason I'm here tonight is to get him hard for you." Michigan popped open the can and set it to his lips, taking a long swallow. "I've done this once before and it went well. Lets them have closure and all that."

Sammi gave him a dirty look. "I don't want closure. I want him to stay."

Michigan reached for Sammi's hands and held them. I moved behind her and set my face in as menacing a grimace as I could. "Miss, I wish keeping him here for you was an option. The ghosts trapped here eventually have problems. Do unexpected things. It makes them crazy staying. You have a unique opportunity to say an actual goodbye. That's why I'm here. That's why I'm pressing to make him hard for you. The beer helps with that. Do you have a private place I can crash? I'll stay out of your way and I'll have drunk enough that you'll have privacy."

No one was asking this man how he was going to get me "hard" and that was what I was the most concerned about.

"What do the brownies do for you?" Sammi tilted her head.

"Nothing. I just eat them." Michigan gave her a

comforting smile.

He was hitting on her. I could feel it.

Finally, Sammi asked the question I was dying to know the answer to. "What does it mean when you say you're going to get him hard?"

I leaned forward so much I was betting my head looked like a turtle sticking out of his shell.

"Well, you know how you can't really touch each other?"

Sammi nodded sadly.

"Well, with me here, I can really focus on him while drinking, and that'll give him permanence. It'll just be this once. It does speed up the whole leaving process, so you have to agree and he has to agree. But I make him hard enough to hug you. Love you. Give you one last night." Michigan dropped Sammi's hands and picked up the first can of beer. He tipped his head back and emptied the contents in a matter of seconds, only swallowing once. He set the can on the counter and cracked the top on the second one.

"I'm going to need to talk to Evan first."

Michigan nodded and sat down on the stepstool that Shark had recently vacated.

Sammi grabbed my hand and it was fully there. Hand on hand. I squeezed and she gasped. She turned to me and felt my chest, her hand slid up, fingertips skimming the side of my neck, causing a wave of goosebumps to cover my skin. I felt suddenly warm, and alive. So, so alive. She cupped my face in both hands and ran her thumbs across my lips. A low moan came from deep within me.

She had tears in her eyes. "Never mind. We don't need to talk. How long do we have?" She gave Michigan a frantic gaze.

"Until morning. That's all I got in me. I'll make him hard for you." And then Michigan stuck an entire brownie in his mouth.

She turned to look at him, and her voice broke. "Thank you."

He nodded and grabbed the remote control. Sammi grabbed my hand and tugged, leading me to the bedroom.

As soon as the door was closed, Sammi started tearing my clothes off. They were real. The same clothes I'd been wearing the night I'd died. The side seam made a splitting sound and Sammi paused her frantic disrobing. "Shit, I don't want to ruin this shirt."

"It's okay, you can ruin it."

She shook her head. "I want it to be in one piece just in case . . . and we both know I can't sew for shit."

"Right." I swallowed hard.

She blew out a breath that I could feel on my skin. When she lifted my shirt this time, she was careful. I tossed the shirt on the floor and wondered if it would disappear along with me come morning. It had looked and felt real.

Sammi stepped into me and rested her cheek against my chest. I wrapped my arms around her and squeezed her tightly.

"I miss you so much already," she whispered.

"Let's just be here, together, and not think about what's going to happen in the morning. Let me love you tonight. I'll fill up your heart." I wanted to make a joke about

filling up other parts of her, but I didn't want to be a tacky asshole.

She nodded against my chest and one of her hands eased down my back until she reached my ass and gave it a squeeze. I waited until she tipped her chin up before I took her face between my palms and bent to kiss her.

It wasn't like the last time we tried this. I was corporeal. I didn't have to do anything but focus on the feel of her lips against mine. She angled her head to the right and I went the other way. Our lips parted and our tongues met. She tasted like cinnamint toothpaste.

I let one hand find her boob and squeezed gently. Sammi moaned and the sound of the TV in the living room grew louder.

"Maybe we should put on some music?" Sammi suggested around my tongue.

"Probably a good idea."

We stopped kissing long enough for her to cue up one of our sex playlists. She turned up the volume, and then we were back to undressing each other. I took my time, which admittedly wasn't something we did much when I was alive.

Usually I would just push her buttons until she went off and then we'd slam into each other like crashing waves. But not this time. I wanted to take my time with her, leave the memory of us engraved on her heart so fucking Michigan couldn't erase it.

"It's just you and me," Sammi whispered, as if she could hear my thoughts.

It wasn't really just the two of us, but I'd take what I

could get. We went back to kissing, softly at first, like first date kisses. Like last kisses.

Sammi gripped my shoulders and sighed. She mumbled something into my mouth that sounded like *best shoulders ever*. Sammi was forever glaring at my shoulders when she was angry. During sex she would take it out on them by leaving nail marks and scratches. I loved it when she got aggressive during our sex battles.

She hopped up and wrapped her legs around my hips like one of those koala bear grippy things. I caught her by two handfuls of ass and carried her over to the bed.

It would be the last time I would get to be with her. I knew that. She knew that. Thankfully, my dick didn't seem to have the sads over it the same way the rest of me did. He was standing proudly and prodding her ass, which was apt considering how often I liked to poke her in the butt with my flesh sword.

When my knees hit the mattress, they made small dents, like I was half real. Sammi glued our mouths back together and tried unbuckling my belt at the same time. I wished I'd been wearing sweatpants when I died, because they were a lot easier to get off.

We got naked the rest of the way and Sammi rolled us over so she could straddle my hips. Her luscious boobs were right there, so I cupped them. I could feel the weight of them in my palms. I brushed a thumb over her nipples and she groaned and rolled her hips.

"I'm going to spend eternity missing this." I followed the dip in her waist down to the flare at her hips.

She shook her head and leaned down. Her long hair

brushed across my chest and my erection jumped on my stomach.

Her lips touched mine and she whispered, "You're not going anywhere without me."

I cupped her cheek in my palm to keep our mouths from connecting. "What the hell is that supposed to mean?"

Her eyes were fiery with defiance. "Don't fight with me right now, Evan." She rolled her hips and cocked a brow.

It made our sex parts line up and I forgot to be pissed off. Our mouths fused and she kept doing that thing with her hips where she would roll them and nestle my hard-on between her folds. I wanted to slow us down. To suspend time and make our last night together last the rest of my non-existence.

I rolled us over so I was on top of her and pushed up on one of my arms. Her gaze went to my shoulder and she sighed and then frowned.

"What's wrong?"

"Nothing."

"My dick is rubbing on your clit and you're frowning. That's not nothing."

"You're flickering. Like a lamp. Sometimes it's like you're really here and then others it's like you're Ghost Evan. I kind of want to coat you in flour so you're easier to see, but that won't taste very good." Her frown deepened for a moment before her eyebrows lifted and so did her lips. "I have an idea!"

"Uh-oh." Sammi's ideas often resulted in me being in questionable scenarios.

"Remember that edible glitter I got for your birthday

last year?"

Of course, I remembered the edible glitter. She'd been on a *Twilight* kick and thought it would be fun for me to role-play Edward. She even made me take a cold shower so my skin was cool and then coated me in edible glitter. The only reason I had said yes was because she'd guaranteed me a blow job. I'd spent the following week trying to get glitter out of places it should never be.

"Didn't you throw it out?"

She shook her head and had the decency to look a little guilty.

"Please? It'll help make all of this feel a little more . . . normal?"

Arguing over the use of edible glitter seemed like a waste of our last night together, so I gave in and let her have at it. She leaned over to the nightstand on her side of the bed and pulled open the bottom drawer. I held onto her bottom to keep her steady.

She opened the tin of silver glitter and dipped her fingers into the shiny semi-liquid and then drew a heart over my heart. "I love you," she whispered.

"I love you, too, babe. More than anything else in the entire world." She brushed silver glitter over the bridge of my nose and along my cheeks. Her fingertips drifted across my lips, down my chin, and along my neck. Over my shoulders and my arms. She made handprints over my chest and my abs. She drew lines down my thighs all the way to the tops of my feet.

And then finally she took my erection in her hand and turned it into a glittering hotdog shaped disco ball. We

kissed and touched. She gave me a mind-blowing blow job and did that thing with her tongue. I returned the favor by spending a small eternity with my face between her thighs.

The best and worst part was not having to take a break to breathe.

The second best part that wasn't even close to the worst was when she yanked on my hair and I felt it.

Eventually, I prowled back up her body and settled between her thighs. We were both covered in glitter. Her lips were silver tinged and puffy. We probably looked like an alien romance gone wrong, but when I slid inside her for what I knew was likely the second last time—I always came twice, back to back—reality smacked me in the face.

I was going to leave her. She would stay here and I would have to go and I didn't want to do that. I didn't want Michigan to replace me. I didn't want to watch her from wherever I was moving on without me. Which I realized was a pretty damn selfish thing to think. But existing while being dead was a real mindfuck.

Sammi's palm had settled against my cheek. "We only have each other for a few more hours. Stay here with me."

We moved together—me mostly corporeal, her alive and warm. We were desperate and sad, in love and terrified of what was coming for us. I made sure she finished first. Her eyes stayed on mine and I saw into her soul—legit I watched it rise out of her half an inch, creating a haze around her that made her seem a little blurry before it settled back under her skin.

"I feel like I just had an out-of-body experience,"

Sammi murmured.

"Even as a ghost I'm the best lay you've ever had." I made a joke. It was all I could do. Otherwise, I was pretty sure I would cry like a baby.

After I came, and she came again, and I came again, we flopped back on the mattress and stared at each other. "You're starting to fade again," she said softly.

She rolled off the bed and crossed over to the bookshelves to pick up a photo album before she returned to bed. The comforter was probably ruined since it was covered in glitter. It would never come out of the sheets. Not that it would matter. Unless she wanted to sleep on these when I was gone. I wondered how long that would last. A week? A month? A year?

Hopefully, she washed them before a year had passed. Or maybe not.

Sammi had been a fan of scrapbooking. But she'd get bored with it about halfway through and never finished them. We had twenty half-full albums and boxes of photos that never made the cut.

She flipped through until she came to a picture of her family. It was one of those really old black and white ones. I stopped her from turning to the next page. I could still do that, but I had to concentrate now where I didn't have to earlier.

"Wait." I pointed to a woman in a long dress, wearing an apron with her hair pulled up on top of her head in a bun. A man stood beside her, their fingers entwined. "That looks like you when you dressed up as Laura Ingalls from *Little House on the Prairie*."

She gave me a look. "I was Anne of Green Gables."

"Close enough. Who is that?" I remembered the conversation I'd had with Morven (not like I'd ever be able to forget it) when he said Sammi had been his before she'd been mine.

"That's my great, great, great aunt Samantha. She died in a horse accident. Got trampled by her own horse on the way down from a trip to Lover's Peak. But I think that was before it was actually Lover's Peak."

I had to wonder if reincarnation was a thing. And if Morven was actually right, that Sammi had been his in another life. I didn't like the thought of that at all.

Sammi flipped through the pages of the album, and I only half paid attention. I stared at her profile and tried to brush a few hairs away from her mouth, but my finger went through her cheek again.

The sky outside was starting to lighten. I'd never been so sad to see a sunrise.

"I want to come with you." Sammi turned to meet my gaze. "If you can't stay, I don't want to stay either."

I didn't want to fight with her to stay. And selfishly, I wanted her to come with me, too. The afterlife seemed like it would suck without her. "What if we don't end up in the same place? What if I go to Hell and you go to Heaven?"

"Then I'll find a way to get to you and you'll find a way to get to me. I don't want to be here without you. Every day will feel like I'm dying."

Existing forever without her would feel a lot like the same.

Twelve

EVAN

WE HAD TO face Morven. And today was yet another noon meeting on Lover's Peak. Michigan offered to drive Sammi, and I was grateful. She sat in the back of his car with me. Michigan looked like he'd had a pretty rough night. He also had a hard time looking either of us in the eye. Sammi had refused to shower before we left, even though it meant she was still smudged with glitter.

She had a small backpack with her and I could offer to hold nothing. We started the climb up. It was a beautiful sunny day again.

"I don't have a good feeling about this." Sammi readjusted her backpack on her shoulders.

I didn't either. Something was coming off the mountain, energy in waves. Bad energy.

"It'll be fine." I rested my hand near her elbow. There was no touching anymore. No matter how hard I tried, I couldn't make it happen. I'd used it all up last night.

"We'll get my body off the mountain. I'll explain that you and your distant relative are two different people while I'm still a ghost. And then it will be good."

She stopped in her tracks, turning to face me, sadder than ever.

She didn't have to say it. I knew. We both knew. This was where our love story ended. I would do my damnedest to convince Morven to leave her alone.

After staring at her hands for a few minutes, she patted her cheeks a little hard and started walking.

She was so goddamn strong. I loved her so much.

When we got to the scene of the crime/top of the mountain, Corbey and Kackley were standing near the cliff, hands on their hips.

"Hey, guys. What's up?" Sammi strode over to them.

"Hey, Miss Riggs. Maybe you should stay over there." They both held up their hands.

Sammi ignored them. I flashed next to her and peered over the edge. The tarp, the cursing chickens, and my body were gone. All gone. As if they never existed.

"Where is it? Where's his body?" Sammi got down to her knees and tried to get a closer look.

"Just stay here. I'll go see what I can find out."

She gave me a small nod. We were getting good at the ghost and woman communication thing. Which was a shame. I flashed down to the cliff. The last time I was there, I was so angry at the bird I didn't pay any attention to my body.

I stood on the thin cliff, and there were no signs of all the activity it had seen in the past few days. The sky got

darker in a way that usually indicated a natural disaster. From sun to gray. From a beautiful temperature to a chilly one.

I glanced up and saw Sammi watching me with her eyes wide. "Behind you!"

She didn't even try to pretend she was doing anything other than shouting a warning to me. I felt him. That creepy essence he had loomed over my spine, my emotions.

I didn't turn. "Morven."

"Annoying dead man." His voice was right behind the shell of my ear.

"What happened to my body? The birds? Everything?" I took baby steps as I turned to face him. Man, I thought I was ready. I was not ready. His limitless echo eyeballs were horrifying. The inside of each like a bottomless pit.

"What happened to my love? The one you were screwing at the top of the mountain to *mock* me?" His voice echoed over and over. He was a stereo ghost.

I held up my hands as if he was a drunk on Tuesday afternoon. "Hey, I was drilling *my* girlfriend, not yours. Did it ever occur to you that you're all messed up in the head? That you've been a ghost so long that you're scrambled? Your love would be long gone. You're so, so old, dude."

He squinted his echo orbs at me. "She's there. I can smell her." He pointed at the top of the cliff with one bony finger.

And he was gone. I flashed so I was right next to Sammi. She scrambled up from her knees and turned to face Morven.

"That's right, always on your knees, taunting me." Morven threw his hands in the air and the mountain got darker. Both Corbey and Kackley backed up, guns drawn, but they had them pointed at the ground.

I wrapped myself around Sammi, my back to Morven. "He's here and he's mad. He thinks you are cheating on him with me. Remember that Michigan said ghosts get mixed up?"

And then I was pulled away from her, not allowed to envelop her in my essence. I was tied—but there were no ropes—to a nearby tree. Morven advanced on Sammi just as the cops were hit with a miniature dirt tornado.

My girl was out there all by herself, and no one was going to be able to help her.

I felt hopeless, when all of a sudden, Morven started flinging his hands around. The rabid raccoons appeared. The pee your pants lightning was summoned. And then, finally, the cursing birds filled the trees.

Michigan stumbled onto the scene. He ran to Sammi and pulled her to his side. Sammi turned toward his chest and buried her face in his sweatshirt. He was in civilian clothes, but still reporting to duty. I was both grateful and hateful at the same time. I couldn't hold her anymore, but at least she had someone with her.

Morven was ramping up again, growing taller and more echoey. His black eye sockets became the size of ponds, his screaming mouth, a river.

I couldn't fight him. I couldn't even get away from this tree. Sammi was doomed, because all Michigan could do was be a human protector.

The ship sailing in on the strong gusts from the sudden storm was huge, old, and fairly majestic. On the bow was a wooden carving of a manatee wearing a wig. Manning the mainsail was Neck Gash and One-Eyed Brains was on the cannon.

I wasn't sure to be filled with dread or hope until Sharkbait screamed, "Fire at will!" to Brains from the helm, jutting his sword in the direction of Morven.

Morven turned his mighty head and let out a horrible laugh as the first ghost cannonball bounced off of his chest like a tennis ball.

Shit.

Michigan was on his phone, shouting out orders and requests for a helicopter while the raccoons surrounded him and the dirt tornado kept the other cops busy. The furry terrors shifted their weight from one back paw to the other, hissing low in their throats.

Corbey and Kackley began yipping as the Urine Bolts started filling their tornado like an ice cream cone.

The birds hooted from the trees in a cacophony of curses.

"Fuckstick sorcerer!"

"Asswip tortoise!"

"Stanky vag goblin!"

And then Morven turned his head toward Sammi. "You *will* be mine again. I will have your soul in the palm of my hand for eternity and you will apologize every second of every day for *ever* letting him," he pointed at me and the birds shouted in chorus, *little pecker*, "touch your lady parts."

There was a moment when Sammi's anger was building that no one recognized but me. When Sammi was about to snap. She had had enough. I'd seen this buildup before. When I threw wet towels on the bed, and more violently when a woman from work sent me a suggestive text she'd meant to go to her husband.

When Sammi was scary, she commanded the room.

"Enough!" she shouted like a fifth grade teacher ten minutes before retirement. "You—I can see you now… you no eyeball having bully!"

She pointed a closed fist in the right direction. The dirt tornado had been tossing a fine dust in Morven's direction. She *could* see him.

Morven paused, maybe catching sight of the giant ghost craft. Sharkbait took the moment to settle his ghost ship near the edge of the cliff and he, Gash, and Brains snuck off the gang plank and onto the mountain while Morven was distracted.

"You cannot give yourself to others. You are *mine*!" Morven was clearly a fucking caveman. Sammi only liked that shit on very specific occasions where there were safewords and velcro.

Sammi lifted her shirt and bra in one defiant movement. "Boobs! Boobs, you giant asshole. I'm giving them to everybody!"

She shook those glorious friends of mine, and there was a deafening silence on the mountain.

Even the birds went quiet, except for one small one. "Pompous slut clown!"

She took the moment to kick more dirt at Morven.

A clump landed right in his eyes. Once he couldn't see boobs anymore, he started to scream. I understood. It was horrible when they went away.

The chaos built around us again.

Sharkbait took on the cursing birds, waving his sword at them to get them to disperse. Gash did his best to redirect the raccoons by running through their ranks. And Brains intercepted the Urine Bolts so the cops could fight their way out of the dirt tornado.

Sammi stormed up to Morven, where she was about as high as his ghost kneecap. "Get the hell down here, you demented bag of wind." She pointed at the spot in front of her.

That was my girl! She told me before she'd go down fighting. I just didn't anticipate having to watch it. I felt tears form in my ghost eyes. Manly, proud ones.

Morven wriggled and twisted, decompressing so he was about the same height as her. He stepped up to Sammi and snaked his arm around her waist. She seemed entranced with his pool eyes and I saw her sway a bit.

"What did you call me?" Morven's ghost voice was now a thunderous whisper. Impossible but potent at the same time.

I watched Sammi throw her shoulders back. "I called you a demented bag of wind! And another thing, I'm about to cry. I always cry when I'm angry, but that doesn't mean what I'm about to say to you has any less value." She put her finger in Morven's face. I struggled hard against whatever was keeping me tied to the tree. It grabbed harder. It almost felt like snakes easing up and down my arms and legs.

Sammi did start crying, her tears big and rolling down her beautiful cheeks. "He wasn't doing anything *to* me. I was *taking* the physical love I consented to from him! I'm not his. I'm not yours. Sweet shit, you old-fashioned asshole!" She started to twist from his grasp, and one of her anger tears flew from her cheek and landed on Morven's face. I watched as the spot turned red and sizzled. Sammi didn't notice, she was on a roll. "And you won't listen worth a damn, but I think you were horny for my great, great, great aunt!"

With every "great" another tear flew onto Morven. His whole face started to sizzle. Her anger tears that she hated so much when we fought were working as actual ammunition against Morven. "And she's been dead a long damn time. And I doubt she'd want to be with a narrow-minded shitshow that insisted women were property. And certainly her ghost has moved on." And then she glowered at him, witnessing her own tear pop and sizzle on Morven like it was a piece of batter getting dropped into hot oil.

"Oh my gosh. You're allergic to my tears! Or something! Rage tears! Oh, you big fart cannon, I've got those for days."

And then Sammi started fight-crying without hindering the flow at all. My girl was tearing up like she was juicing her eyeballs. Morven was popping and sizzling. The manly ghost tears that I felt in my eyes I let flow and drip onto the snakes that were holding me. They reacted similarly, popping and sizzling until I could free myself.

Once I could run, I went to Sammi and started flinging

my own tears at Morven as well.

He writhed and cowered from us. Shark saw what was happening, and he was able to toss a tear or two at the raccoons and they started scurrying away.

"Feel yer wounds, boys! And flick those tears like boogers at these buggers!"

Morven got smaller and smaller until he was the size of a soccer ball. I picked him up and held him out to Sammi.

He held out his bony arms, trying to shield what was left of his body from her.

"I've been defeated by a bunch of crybabies! How is that even possible?" tiny Morven howled.

Sammi was able to sprinkle a few more tears on him until he was no bigger than a bottlecap. I clamped my ghost hands around him to trap him and we looked for something to put him in.

"Look at this. A condom." She picked a wrapped condom up off the ground.

The cops were busy trying to wineberry the raccoons out of the area as Sammi and I opened the condom and stuffed Morven inside.

"You can haunt a weiner wrapper for the rest of your days." I shook the condom a little and watched him bounce around. When my grip was getting tenuous, Sammi took him from me and stuck him in her pocket.

Soon after Morven was in Sammi's pocket, the horrible storm piddled out. The birds settled into the trees and the raccoons disappeared into the surrounding thicket.

It was almost quiet, and I felt myself slipping. Sammi was talking to Michigan, the helicopter's blades were stirring up the dust, and the very atoms that held me together started to vibrate. Sharkbait was next to me.

"Hey, ghost brother. You stay here long enough and you won't be here for long." He pointed to the gangplank of his ghost ship. The manatee bow's boobs were resting on the cliff.

"What about her?" I couldn't take my eyes off of Sammi as she laughed at something Michigan said.

"She's going to live a long, happy life, if she's lucky. You took the fall off that cliff for her, and now it's time to let go."

I didn't have a ghost to fight, but I had plenty of tears. Gash and Brains were already lumbering back to the ship.

"What happened to my body?"

"We don't know. But we also have never seen a ghost linger so long after it's been gone. You must love her something fierce."

"Almost as fierce as she is." I wiped at my eyes and then held out a hand to Sharkbait. "Thank you for all your help. Good luck with your mermaid. I'm staying here— looking at her until I can't anymore."

Sammi turned and scanned the area for me. Our gazes met. I couldn't leave her.

Epilogue

SAMMI

IT HAD BEEN two years since the ghost battle. I wrote about my experiences, framed them as fiction, and got Lover's Peak a ton of new tourists. We used the funds to rehab the rabid raccoons and get them dental care, teach the birds curse words in many different languages, and establish a clinic for people with bladder control issues, utilizing the bolts.

I say we, and I meant Evan and me. Yes, he's still a ghost. Yes, we still fought. But we were able to take Lover's Peak and make it something that brought people together. We championed the local powers that be for guardrails to keep visitors and selfie takers safe. We even built a few lovers' cabins for those fighting couples that couldn't take their hands off each other. We bought almost the entire mountain for a song because it had such a horrible reputation for being haunted.

And it was haunted. Michigan was a good friend, and

he would drop by with a six pack of beer and brownies a few times a month. We weren't sure why his powers lasted. That was a mystery as well as where Evan's body had gone.

We learned that a semi-famous pirate's remains were up for sale, and we purchased them. Sharkbait was thrilled to be reunited with his body because his mermaid love had gone belly up about six months ago. Her body was even caught in a giant whirlpool in the ocean, much like a toilet bowl being flushed. Her ghost appeared alongside him on his ghost ship, and she was indeed a manatee in a wig. Gash and Brains were long gone, having found some sense in the ghost battle and deciding to give up bullying and find out what the next life had in store for them. They were disgusting to look at, and it was quite nice to have them gone.

We never found Evan's body, but I had a hunch that Shark had moved it so Evan could have a chance, no matter how slim, to stay with me on Lover's Peak.

One day, forty-five years in the future, I would die in Ghost Evan's arms and we would go on the next hike hand in hand. Together booever.

THE END

Acknowledgements

Together we would like to say thank you to our readers for letting us be silly, our families for letting us be silly and for our sweet friends for putting up with our silly. Tijan, for going in on this Halloween thing with us.

CP Smith

Christina Santos

Sarah Piechuta

Debra's Beta Girls

Helena's Hustlers

Gel Ytayz from Tempting Illustrations

Social Butterfly

Jenn Watson

TJ Designs for the cover & graphics!

Kimberly Brower

Aimee Ashcraft

About The Author Helena Hunting

NYT and USA Today bestselling author, Helena Hunting lives on the outskirts of Toronto with her incredibly tolerant family and two moderately intolerant cats. She writes contemporary romance ranging from new adult angst to romantic sports comedy.

About The Author Debra Anastasia

#1 in humor and Amazon top 40 bestselling author, Debra Anastasia lives on the outskirts of Maryland with her incredibly lactose intolerant family and two moderately incontinent pets. She writes contemporary romance ranging from new adult angst to the weirdest crap you've ever read.

For more information visit DebraAnastasia.com. And if you loved this book, leaving a review is the equivalent of making a ghost hard. Thank you so much for reading.